World of Reading

The Best TREE HOUSE Ever

Written by
Laura Buller

Illustrated by the
AMEET Studio Artists

 For information address Disney Press, 1200 Grand Central Avenue, Glendale, California 91201.
First Paperback Edition, June 2019
1 3 5 7 9 10 8 6 4 2
ISBN 978-1-368-02681-9
FAC-029261-19116
Library of Congress Control Number: 2018966571
Printed in the United States of America
For more Disney Press fun, visit www.disneybooks.com

There is a girl who loves to build with her LEGO bricks.

She built all the princess castles. Then she put them together. She made a big new castle. It is magical.

The girl loves the Disney Princesses, too. She put them in the castle. Now she makes up stories about them.

This is one of her stories. . . .

“Aha! Here is the last piece of butterfly!” says Aurora.

The princesses are finishing a puzzle. It is game night in the magical castle. They love being together and playing games.

Cinderella gives Mulan a high five. “Nothing puzzles us, right?”

Mulan looks for the puzzle box to tidy up. Oh, no! The puppy is chewing on a puzzle piece.

"Paws off that puzzle, please!" she says, laughing. "We will take you for a walk soon."

Rapunzel turns to her friends and asks, "Can I take the puppy out alone?"

Mulan wonders why Rapunzel wants to be alone. She leads her to the chair by the fireplace.

"Is something wrong?" Mulan asks quietly while the other princesses play with the puppy. "Are you unhappy?"

Rapunzel smiles at her kind friend. “I am very happy here. I love you all like sisters. I never had a sister!”

She says, “But sometimes I just need a little alone time.”

“To let your hair down?” Mulan jokes.

Mulan hugs her friend. "Take the puppy for a walk, and let me think! I want to help you."

Rapunzel heads out the castle door with the puppy. She is smiling again. She knows her friend will help!

As soon as Rapunzel is far enough away, Mulan calls out, "Princess meeting!"

The princesses get together. Mulan explains that their friend needs to be alone sometimes.

So the princesses make a plan to build a tree house in the garden.

Then Rapunzel can be alone without going too far away from her friends.

The princesses decide to keep the plan a secret from Rapunzel. So, when she returns with the puppy, they send her on some errands.

"We're nearly out of fish food for the pond!" says Ariel.

"And birdseed for the feeder!" adds Snow White.

Rapunzel wonders why she has to do everything, but she is always happy to help her friends.

Rapunzel is gone. Time to get started! Aurora is the best at climbing trees. She finds the perfect spot in one to build a tree house.

Aurora ties a rope around the sturdy tree trunk. She lowers a basket, and Mulan fills it up with wood. The puppy tries to get in the basket, too!

Mulan climbs up into the tree. They start to build the tree house. Jasmine has made a list of instructions.

This is not so tricky, Mulan thinks. *If we can build the best friendships, we can build a great tree house!*

Meanwhile, Rapunzel runs her errands. She smiles to herself. *It is wonderful to have good friends,* she thinks. *But it's also nice to be alone!*

Back at the castle, the
tree house is nearly done.
All the princesses have
worked hard.

“What this tree house needs,” says Mulan, “is the princess touch.”

The princesses decorate the walls and roof. They add pictures of flowers and animals. The puppy barks and runs in a circle. Rapunzel is coming!

Rapunzel is confused. There is no one in the castle. Where are her friends? She thinks they must be outside.

“Hello, puppy!” says Rapunzel. “Where is everyone?”

She hears a giggle and a “Shhh!” in the treetops. Then she hears a big “SURPRISE!”

And what a surprise! Her friends are waving to her from a beautiful tree house.

"We want you to be happy here forever," Mulan says. "So when you need some time alone, away from everything, this is a special place for you."

"Of course, there is room to invite us over, too!" Belle says with a laugh. "No ballroom, though!"

Rapunzel smiles up at her wonderful friends.

"I love it. Thank you so much!" says Rapunzel. "I can hide away here, but I'll never be too far from the best friends ever."